Designers: Emily Muschinske

Cover Design: Michaela Zanzani

Cover illustration and interior illustration on page 16 by Yancey Labat

Special thanks to Marvel: Ruwan Jayatilleke,

Jeff Poulin, Carl Suecoff, and James Hinton.

Published by Scholastic Inc., 557 Broadway,
New York, NY 10012, by arrangement with Marvel Entertainment, Inc.
SCHOLASTIC and associated logos are trademarks and/or registered
trademarks of Scholastic Inc.

ISBN 0-439-92699-8

12 11 10 9 8 7 6 5 4 3 2 1   7 8 9 10 11 12/0

Printed in the U.S.A.
First Scholastic printing, January 2007

Table of Contents

4

CHAPTER ONE

Blinding white light bounded from the endless expanse of the Arizona desert, searing the Abomination's eyes and baking his lizard-like skin. Raising a tracking device, he studied a fast-approaching blip and grinned like a leering green dragon. Squinting, he could almost see the bus in the far distance that carried his prize.

"Well, what do you know..." the Abomination murmured. "The kid's on time." The Abomination was waiting for thirteen-year-old Bobby Phillips. Bobby was on a bus from Tucson, heading to Los Angeles to spend the summer with relatives. He had no idea what kind of trouble he was getting himself into.

Pocketing the tracker, the seven-foot-tall, one-ton menace prepared to attack.

The Hulk was lonely and bored. Sitting atop a towering stone spire, the raging afternoon sun beating down on his back, he dimly remembered the many times he had hollered, "Hulk just want to be left alone!"

Now he was all by himself. No one hounded him. No one wanted to fight him. No one called him a monster. For five long days—not that he had a clear sense of the passage of time—Hulk had not seen another living soul.

He'd played toss with boulders in magnificent ravines. He'd spent hours leaping high, trying to reach the soft, puffy clouds in the sky. He had chowed down on cactus, raced the wind, and drank from river streams.

He'd been so happy at first, but now he wanted someone to play with, and something to do.

"Hulk bored now," he murmured.

A rumbling echoed from the desert. Hulk looked down and saw a big, blue metal tin can winding its way across a road, evading big rocks and potholes. Excitement rose in his heart. *Maybe people were inside the tin can, and some of them might want to be Hulk's friends!*

Hulk shuddered. No. Humans couldn't be trusted. All they did was hound Hulk, and try to hurt him. Better he ignore the shiny metal thing until it was lost from sight. Hanging his head sadly, Hulk looked away.

If he had watched a moment longer, he would have seen the Abomination burst from behind a large stone and race right at the bus!

Bobby Phillips loved his tunes. He sat five rows back in the nearly empty bus bound for Los Angeles, head bobbing and heavy boots tapping to the rhythm.

A rangy old man dressed in black denim scratched his long beard and grinned at Bobby from across the aisle. Bobby had to take out an earphone to hear what the man was saying.

"I said," repeated the man, "you like music?"

The man in black nodded at a guitar case jammed in the seat next to him. "Long way to LA. If you want, I could give you some lessons to make the time go faster. I used to be in a band!"

Bobby flashed him a toothy grin. "That's okay. I love music but...I'm just more into drawing."

"Hey, that's great!" said the old-timer.

Nodding, Bobby recalled the trouble at school and why he was being shipped off to his military brat cousins in LA. *Not everybody thinks what I do is so great...*

Before he could dwell on it a second longer, the bus suddenly swerved. The driver struck the brakes hard.

SCREEEEECH!

Something plowed into the vehicle! Bobby was thrown from his seat. Tumbling end over end, he heard rending metal, saw the sky suddenly spring into view, and realized the bus had been torn in two!

Then someone—or some*thing*—grabbed at him. He saw a nightmarish face, part lizard, part man, and heard crazy laughter.

And his wildly skidding world went black. 🔘

CHAPTER TWO

Hulk was on his feet the instant he heard the crash. Whirling, he saw the bus sawed in half, each section skidding to a stop in different directions. Dazed people stumbled from the wreckage, limping and startled, but not seriously hurt.

Standing in the road, holding a young boy high in the blazing heat, stood a figure the Hulk knew all too well. Knew...and did not like.

"Where is it?!" screamed the Abomination. "Hand it over and you won't get hurt...much."

The boy shook his head as he came around, his backpack ripping down the side. "What are you talking about?"

"Fine," the Abomination said. "We'll do this the hard way...."

11

"Abomination!" Hulk screamed. "Hulk smash Abomination!"

The green goliath leaped high into the air, his great feet poised to plunge at the Abomination's massive, scaly back. But as the the Hulk was about to land, his enemy whirled, tossed the boy away, and drove a fist up at the underside of the Hulk's jaw.

The explosive blow was as loud and shattering as an unexpected thunderclap. Hulk hit the ground hard, digging a long sandy ditch in the earth. He spat out sand and rock, roared, and faced a roundhouse punch that might have staggered him had he not been ready for it.

The Abomination pummeled Hulk with a series of relentless blows that sent the green-skinned, gamma-irradiated giant smashing into a

huge standing stone.

Hulk roared and growled. Sweat poured in Hulk's eyes, salty and stinging.

"Now you make Hulk angry!" Hulk bellowed. "And the madder Hulk gets, the stronger he gets!"

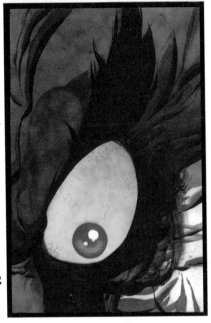

Hulk launched himself at the Abomination with the force of an exploding star. The Abomination grunted and howled in fury as the Hulk's huge fists came at him. Hulk's strong uppercut lifted the Abomination off his feet and sent him a dozen yards into the air.

The monster plummeted to the ground and struck with the force of a meteor hitting the earth.

The Hulk roared and screamed, "Hulk is strongest one there is!"

Footsteps ground in the sand at Hulk's back. He spun, chest heaving—and looked down at the boy the Abomination had snatched from the bus.

"You saved me," the boy said, smiling with admiration and thanks—and not a trace of fear.

Hulk stared at the lad in confusion. Out of the corner of his eye, he saw the other people from the bus pointing at him. They were yelling, "Monster!"

"I heard that you take giant leaps that go miles at a time," the boy said. "Is that true?"

Hulk scratched the side of his forehead. He tried to think about what the boy had asked, tried to reason, but it just made Hulk's head hurt.

"You okay," Hulk said. "Hulk go now."

Just as Hulk was about to leap away, he heard the Abomination rising from the dust.

"Boy!" howled the Abomination. "You will give me what I've come for. No one can stop me. No one can protect you—not even the Hulk!"

The young teenager adjusted his baseball

cap. "Um, Hulk? My name's Bobby. Bobby Phillips. You think you can give me a lift?"

Hulk hesitated—then held out his hand. "Boy really not afraid of Hulk?"

Bobby shrugged. "Should I be?"

Hulk shook his head. "No. Hulk save boy."

The Abomination stalked closer.

"Well then, buddy," Bobby said as he took Hulk's hand. "Let's make like a banana and split!"

Hulk hesitated, looking around. "Bananas? Hulk like bananas."

Realizing his mistake, Bobby said anxiously, "I mean—let's go!"

"Oh," Hulk said. Sweeping Bobby onto his back, Hulk took a running start and leaped high into the sky.

Below, the Abomination howled, but in seconds the sound of the wind drove away the monster's cries as the pair rushed at the clouds.

CHAPTER THREE

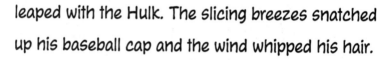

"**W**oo-hoo!"
Bobby
hollered as he
leaped with the Hulk. The slicing breezes snatched
up his baseball cap and the wind whipped his hair.

The Hulk's mighty form plunged to the ground,
struck hard, and bounded up to the sky again.
Bobby's stomach lurched as he held on tightly to
the Hulk's neck. His backpack, jammed to the
brim, bounced and shifted with every impact.
Bobby hoped nothing would fall out.

Good thing I didn't eat yet! he thought.

Soon, the green-skinned giant landed on the
ledge of a mammoth cave. There were tooth-like
stalactites and stalagmites everywhere. Bobby
felt like he was stepping into the hungry jaws

of some great beast. But with Hulk at his side, he wasn't afraid.

"Animals not come here," Hulk proudly proclaimed. "This Hulk's house!"

Bobby nodded, holding his breath as Hulk squeezed by him.

He was grateful beyond words to the Hulk, but the big guy sure gave off one heck of a stench.

They wandered deep into the cave. Bobby was thrilled to hear a trickling stream in the cave's deeper depths. He ran to it, dipped his hands into the cool water, and drank.

The Hulk knelt down beside him and plunged his face in, splashing Bobby. The boy jumped back as Hulk took several big gulps and then came up for air, his face dripping.

"Hulk not thirsty anymore," the behemoth said.

Laughing, Bobby ran his hand through his moistened hair and said, "Me neither."

Stretching his legs, Bobby looked around the cave. He smelled something rank and spotted the remains of a cactus the Hulk had been chowing down on. Next to it, he saw a handful of items: blankets, a busted TV, and a big, silly-looking, rubber toy bear that appeared to have been squeezed pretty hard a couple of times.

He's like a big kid, Bobby realized. *A big kid who could bench-press a football stadium...*

"Hulk find stuff at shack where no one live anymore," Hulk explained, as he pointed at the items he had scavenged. "He hoped for ice cream and cake, but not find any. Hulk kinda sad...then Hulk squeeze bear, and Hulk feel better."

Nodding, Bobby drew his cell phone from his back pocket and tried to get a signal, but, as he feared, the phone was broken.

19

"Hulk, do you know other places where people used to be—maybe still are and might have phones? I need to let my folks know I'm okay. Don't want them worrying."

Hulk's expression darkened. "You don't want to stay with Hulk?"

Bobby grinned. "To be honest, I kinda would rather spend the summer hanging out with you than with my military brat cousins. But one way or the other, I need to call my folks. They've been through enough on account of me, I guess...."

Hulk frowned. "You do something bad?"

With a shrug, Bobby said, "People think I did. Lots of them. A lot who should know better."

Hulk nodded. "Puny humans always think Hulk bad. But Hulk not do anything...."

Bobby looked away. "Yeah. Seems like we've got a lot in common. I just like minding my own business and having fun. But, um...well, for now, I need to find out why the Abomination's after me. He thinks I've got something, and I have no idea what that might be!"

Hulk yawned. Talking always made him tired. He stretched, his rank radioactive armpits emitting even nastier smells than before!

That does it, Bobby thought. He unslung his backpack and looked for his deodorant. Suddenly, the tear in the bag ripped wider and all his music disks spilled onto the cave floor.

"Oh, no!" Bobby said. "All my cool mixes!"

His sketch pads sped out next. Several flopped open to reveal scenes he had drawn in Tucson. Hulk crouched low and looked at the pictures while Bobby gathered up his disks.

"Hulk like pictures," said the Hulk. "You draw picture of Hulk?"

Bobby grinned. "You bet. I—"

His fingers froze on a strange silver disk. Bobby picked it up and examined it in the beam of reflected sunlight. "I've never seen this before. It's got some weird writing on it...some kind of code or a foreign language."

Bobby suddenly remembered an incident at the bus stop that morning. A strange man wearing sunglasses had knocked over Bobby's open backpack. The man had insisted on helping him with it. The bus pulled up and when he looked back, the man was gone. Then two other suspicious-looking people in dark suits hurried by. One was a tall man with long green hair, the other a petite brunette.

"That guy must have planted this disk on me!" Bobby said. "Like in a spy movie. There's a government research facility across town. Maybe this disk came from there!" He searched his bag and found a case with a strange, black device in its corner. "This is how they're tracking the disk!"

Suddenly, Hulk sniffed the air and looked up sharply. The Abomination was standing in the cave mouth holding a cannon.

"Hulk smash!" roared the green-skinned hero. The enemy raised the cannon. "Not likely."

A sudden flood of emerald-and-gold energies burst from the weapon and struck the Hulk head-on. He was driven back into the cave. Green-and-yellow lightning whipped about him as the Abomination pressed forward.

"A gamma-tech gun," the Abomination proclaimed. "It robs you of your strength by absorbing the radiation in your body. I was a scientist, too, as your alter ego, Dr. Bruce Banner, knows. But I retained my intelligence and continued my research—"

"Hey!" Bobby hollered. "Frog face!"

The Abomination whipped toward the boy.

"Made ya look," Bobby said. He held a

heavy stone over the disk. "Let him go or I smash the disk!"

The Abomination laughed. "You have courage, boy. I'll give you that. But you're not as smart as you think—or as observant. Look around you."

Bobby tensed as a half dozen men wearing green-and-black uniforms peeled from the shadows. One knocked the stone from his hand before he could smash the disk, and two others seized his arms and legs.

"HYDRA command?" said the Abomination, as he opened a communicator. "I have the disk, and an unexpected bonus...."

Bobby struggled, but could do nothing to stop the Abomination and his men as they clamped huge chains on the stunned Hulk and dragged both their captives from the cave.

CHAPTER FOUR

The Hulk stirred, his muddled mind awakening slowly. Glaring light greeted him and he felt weak and strange. Hulk tried to move, tried to bellow as a sudden rage consumed him, but something stopped him. Shining blue-white energies surrounded him, binding him. He was in a cage! Yes, he recognized that, now. A cage made of bright light that sapped his strength. Beyond the cage, Hulk spied gleaming silver metal walls and puny humans wearing long white coats. Some of them were talking.

"I don't understand why he hasn't reverted to Banner," one scientist growled.

"Banner?" asked a second.

The first shook his head. "Didn't you read his file? The Hulk is research scientist Bruce Banner. He became the Hulk when he was exposed to intense gamma rays from a weapon of his own design. The army was testing it in the desert when someone wandered onto the site. He would have been killed if not for Dr. Banner's self-sacrifice. He's quite the hero, especially considering the price he's paid ever since."

"You mean becoming the Hulk?" asked the second. "A monster?"

"Yes," replied the first. "This is very odd. We've drained so much radiation from him, yet he won't change back to his human form. Perhaps in time. Then we can study him better...."

Hulk saw the pair walk off. He hadn't understood much of what they had said. All he knew was that he wanted to escape this prison. He wanted to know where the boy had been taken. And the mention of that hated name, Banner, was filling him with an even greater rage. He also hated being called a monster.

And whenever the Hulk grew angrier, he also grew stronger.

Hulk thrust his hands forward, attempting to push through his cage. He didn't make it and his failure frustrated him that much more. That frustration powered his anger and caused even greater strength to flow through him. He thrust again and this time his hands flew even farther.

Soon he would be free! Then he would find the boy—and smash his enemies.

Hulk opened his mouth to roar, and this time, a low, threatening growl emerged. Soon. Soon...

Bobby sat in a metal chair in a far corner across from the Hulk's holding cell. A guard stood near him, but otherwise, he hadn't been handcuffed or secured to the chair.

I guess they don't see me as trouble, Bobby thought, forcing away a grin. He recalled all the speeches he'd had to sit through recently—from the school principal and counselors, to his parents, to a handful of civic leaders. Any of them would be quick to tell these guys that Bobby was nothing but trouble.

Outside Hulk's cave, a huge, hovering metal barge had been waiting, and that's where they had been taken. The guys in the green-and-black costumes referred to it as a "helicarrier." From what Bobby could tell, this "HYDRA" that the Abomination had mentioned was a large organization of spies and other criminals bent on taking over the world.

They're the bad guys, thought Bobby. *And that Abomination creep is working for them. Whatever's on that disk is going to help them achieve their crazy goal...and pretty soon, too!*

They have to be stopped.

Bobby heard the Hulk's low, muffled growls. The guard watching Bobby, the only one left in the room at that moment, whirled on the green goliath in surprise. Hulk was battering away at his cage, and would soon be free!

The guard reached toward an alarm panel on the wall. But before he could reach it, Bobby snatched a metal tray from a nearby table

and brought it down on the guard, knocking him out cold!

Then Bobby raced to the Hulk's holding cell. He desperately scanned the area for controls that would help him release his friend, but there were so many banks of flashing lights, keypads, and keyboards, he didn't know what to do! The machines were shaped like hourglasses, with long glowing rods and spirals of energy snaking across them. *How am I going to shut them all down?* thought Bobby.

From within the glowing cage, Hulk snarled, "Smash. Hulk smash!"

"You know, big guy?" Bobby said. "That's not a bad idea!"

Bobby raised the tray again and

brought it down on all the machinery. Great bursts of shattering sparks rose up and flew all around him. Bobby heard the sound of running footfalls, and people hollering at him to stop. Then strong hands were on him, dragging him from the Hulk's cage. Someone wrested the tray from him: a man wearing a green-and-black HYDRA uniform.

"Kid, you've done it now!" the agent snarled.

Everyone froze in their tracks. Bobby looked beyond the suddenly terrified HYDRA agents and saw the glowering emerald face of his friend.

The Incredible Hulk was free!

CHAPTER FIVE

Hulk's heavy fist swept out and the HYDRA agents tumbled like bowling pins. Enraged, Hulk leveled all the equipment that had powered his cage—simply because it was there.

"Puny humans!" Hulk hollered. "No one is stronger than Hulk!"

Surging forward, Hulk tore the door to the research lab from its hinges and thundered into the hall. He was dimly aware of the boy hurrying behind him, calling to him. But all he cared about was finding the Abomination—and smashing him!

Dozens of HYDRA agents flooded into the hall ahead of the Hulk. Some raced ahead of the others and dropped to their knees, forming two neat military rows. Every one of them raised shiny silver weapons and prepared to fire.

Without slowing his stride, Hulk grinned and clapped his hands together with such explosive force that a shock wave rippled out and sent the enemy agents flying back. Hulk stormed forward and called, "Abomination! Come fight Hulk! Hulk show you who's stronger!"

Suddenly, Bobby tore out from behind the Hulk. "Listen to me. We've got to get that disk and get out of here. Forget about the Abomination!"

Hulk hesitated, his brow wrinkling in the difficult act of concentration, and looked down at the boy.

"The disk!" Bobby cried. "The, um...the shiny round thing I had in my bag, with my sketchbooks."

Hulk nodded slowly. "Pictures good."

More running footsteps came from the corridor up ahead.

Hulk squeezed his hands into fists, anticipating the battle. "Smashing better!"

The ceiling exploded in a shower of flaming shards and a reptilian hand shot down from above and snagged Bobby's jacket. Before Hulk could make a move, the yelping teenager was hauled away. With a roar, Hulk leaped up to follow, landing flat on the deck of the HYDRA helicarrier.

Before him lay the leering face of the Abomination.

"You'll never see that disk again," the Abomination promised. "Even as we speak, the information it contains is being decoded and uploaded to our international servers."

Hulk had no idea what the Abomination was talking about. All he understood was that his enemy had the boy, and so long as he did, Hulk was powerless to fight him.

Hulk threw his head back and bellowed in rage. He brought his massive fists down on the helicarrier deck, smashing through the hull and sending more shock waves through the craft. Hulk's attack sent the craft scraping against the side of the mountain.

Furious, Hulk charged at a group of approaching HYDRA agents. They scattered, several leaping overboard to fall to the churning river below.

Chest heaving, Hulk shouted, "Hulk smash!"

Still dangling from the Abomination's iron grip, Bobby pointed at a tower topped by a satellite dish. "Hulk, forget about me. Destroy that tower! It's going to broadcast the information that was on the disk. Smash it! Smash everything if you've got to!"

"Don't even think about it, Hulk!" yelled the Abomination, as his fingers closed on the boy's throat.

Hulk gripped the sides of his skull.

He didn't know what to do and trying to think so much made his head hurt!

Dropping to his knees, he let out a chilling roar and smashed his fists down in frustration!

"Wha—" began the Abomination as the deck rippled beneath him. The monster teetered on his toes and his grip eased just enough for Bobby to wriggle free and drop to the deck.

"Go, Hulk, go!" Bobby hollered.

Looking up sharply, Hulk saw the Abomination reaching for his friend once more. Hulk rocketed at his enemy. Landing a barrage of punches on the dragon-man, Hulk drove the Abomination back. They soared across the deck, knocking down HYDRA agents, wrecking helicopters and ground vehicles, and smashing cannons. Two tons of rippling, gamma-irradiated muscle and bulk skidded to within a few inches of the communications tower. And stopped.

The Abomination struck at the Hulk,

slamming him back, and sprang to his feet. He snagged a chunk of debris and aimed it like a javelin at the thirteen-year-old.

"You were warned," the Abomination shouted. "Both of you!"

WHOOOSH

ZINGGG!

Before Hulk could leap into action, the Abomination hurled the half-ton of debris right at Bobby!

40

CHAPTER SIX

In all the confusion, Hulk had been unaware of the steady beating of a helicopter's wings from above the helicarrier. He hadn't seen the pair of plunging figures descending from above: a musclebound man with bright green hair and a petite woman who transformed in midair into the green-skinned, green-haired She-Hulk!

The super heroes, She-Hulk and Doc Samson, struck the deck in front of Bobby an instant before the debris reached him. Samson whirled and shielded Bobby while She-Hulk gave the incoming debris a powerful roundhouse punch.

WHAM!

A hailstorm of shrieking, twisted metal flew back at the villainous Abomination.

42

He put his arms up and bellowed as the debris hit him hard.

The Hulk looked on in wide-eyed wonder. *Were Samson and She-Hulk friends or enemies?*

She-Hulk laughed as the Abomination shuddered and hauled the debris from him. "Come on, Bronksi, or Abomination—whichever you'd rather be called. Did you really think you were the only one tracking that disk? How about the folks your group stole it from?"

The Hulk seized the Abomination. "Hulk smash ugly Abomination!"

"I think that's our cue to take off," Samson said, as he put his hand on Bobby's shoulder.

"Not yet," She-Hulk said. "Bobby was right. We have to stop them from broadcasting the rest of that signal and decoding—"

Hulk roared and slammed the Abomination back through the communications tower, wrecking the satellite dish! Hulk had no

idea that destroying the tower was a good thing. It was just the closest thing to smash.

"Never mind," She-Hulk said. "Now really is a good time to head for the hills."

"But, wait!" Bobby cried. "Hulk, he—"

"He's having fun," Samson said with a grin, as he nodded at the green-skinned goliath.

It was true. Hulk had the Abomination by the ankle and was sweeping him around in wide, dizzying arcs. More HYDRA agents abandoned ship, either in antigravity emergency crafts or simply by leaping overboard.

The airship rammed hard into the side of the mountain as the Hulk and the Abomination continued to battle. Hulk pounded his foe down into the belly of the craft. The Abomination in turn punched Hulk through the hull and used him to tear the ship in half!

The two halves of the helicarrier spiraled down into the river. The Hulk and the Abomination roared and fought until the ship splashed down and vanished from sight.

Meanwhile, She-Hulk, Samson, and Bobby watched from a cliff overlooking the ravine.

"Oh, Bruce," She-Hulk said sadly.

Samson smiled. "Don't worry, he'll be fine. He always is."

SPLASH!

Suddenly, a burst of water rose from below, and the Hulk leaped from the river. He landed on the ledge beside the others and stepped between She-Hulk and Bobby.

"Boy Hulk's friend," Hulk said. "Protect boy!"

"You don't have to protect him from us, Bruce," She-Hulk said softly. "Don't you remember me? It's Jennifer. Your cousin."

Hulk flinched. "Hulk is Hulk. Not puny Banner! Hulk is strongest one of all!"

Bobby looked past the Hulk. Down below, he saw the Abomination wobble out of the water on unsteady legs, and then plop facedown on the shore, out cold.

Hulk looked to Bobby. "Boy stay?"

"Hulk, I told you," Bobby said. "I've got to talk with my folks. They probably heard what happened to the bus. They're going to be worried." Bobby ran his hand through his hair. "See...they think I painted some graffiti at school. I didn't. Someone stole one of my sketchbooks and planted it there. But I never even tried to defend myself. I just got mad at the people who should have defended me, but didn't. I have to go back home and stand up for myself, like I did with the Abomination—like the way you do when people accuse you of doing bad things."

Hulk held out his hands. "But...Hulk not want to be alone."

"Then come back with us," Samson offered. "I bet you could stay with the Avengers or the Fantastic Four."

Hulk took a step back. "No...this trick. Boy promise to make picture of Hulk."

"I will," Bobby said. "In fact, if I had my sketch pad, I'd do it right now. But I'd rather we wait until we get to hang out again next time—if that's okay with you."

Hulk beamed. "Boy is Hulk's friend!"

Bobby nodded—and hugged the Hulk! He pinched his nose and tried not to flinch when the Hulk squeezed back hard.

Bobby looked back to Samson and

She-Hulk. "So what was on that disk anyway?"

She-Hulk raised an eyebrow. "Well, if you had the right security clearance I might tell you that it contained plans for a force shield barrier large enough to protect an entire city from any kind of attack. A shield that would make whoever owned it invincible. But you don't have that clearance, so all I can say is…it's classified." She winked.

Bobby laughed. "Cool!"

The Hulk and Bobby said their farewells just before She-Hulk and Samson's rescue helicopter arrived.

The Hulk leaped away, but this time, Hulk's heart was light. He knew that he would never truly be alone as long as he had friends.